KRAMPUS' CHRISTMAS BRIDE

A MONSTER BRIDES PARANORMAL ROMANCE

RAVEN HUSH

First Edition

Cover design by Kit Fox

ISBN Ebook: 978-1-922448-81-1

ISBN Paperback: 978-1-922448-82-8

CONTENT WARNING

Krampus' are, by nature, tricky creatures. It turns out that this particular one loves to tame a good brat, a little pain and is a total assh– I mean, a sadist. Devlin and Tanya's story has dark themes, including harsh language, death, gore and other fun fluids play (use your imagination and we're there), as well as delving into the world of BDSM. There is also some suicide ideation and a history of cutting. The author does not condone or romanticize these ideals.

Please read safely, and enjoy your Krampus with a side serve of soot and birchwood.

Raven

PS - the plural of Krampus is Krampusse. You'll need that later.

for boys' weekends
because I write more on those

CHAPTER ONE

DEVLIN

I sit across from my date and smile into my coffee mug in a way that brings a pretty strain to her cheeks. The girl—an adult in every sense of the word though still many centuries younger than I am —let me have a second date with her, and that, in her short history, is unheard of.

Just as a Krampus stalker like myself should know.

You see, Tanya Hinson is on the naughty list. *My* naughty list.

Not that she knows it, but watching her flit from date to date in the coffee shop beneath her apartment like her online contacts are her personal flirt bar brews something within me I know I should never let roam free.

Except Christmas is the season I love to hate... and unluckily for her, it's here.

Self control is never something I've worried about, much like my present-tossing brother who exists off the joy people throw into the atmosphere for a few meager days of the year.

My existence absorbs emotion on a much darker scale.

And Christmas week in San Francisco, a full three days until my big bro's big day, is the prime time to screw around and find out. Twins, born of the same soul and split, like a sunbeam and its shadowy accompaniment. Only I'm not irrevocably linked to my sibling. While Saint Nick is out making all the good offspring of humanity happy, I focus on those a little older, and activities a whole lot... filthier.

The old pamphlets that used to send Europe into a flurry about the horned devil terrorizing children were really just me with a little spanking habit and a whole lot of satisfied wives who wouldn't know what true pleasure was if I didn't visit them on an annual basis.

I mean, a Krampus should share the love, and all.

After a while I became tired of being hunted by cuckolded husbands, and the demands of otherwise unsated housewives addicted to my form of pleasure who got to call themselves a princess while they rode my cock once a year. Then humanity fell into a cesspit of wars so entangled with their own egos that I hid away from the world entirely, and chose to terrorize a few otherworldly creatures for the duration.

When I emerged, I found the world changed, though the people were...different.

The housewives came into their own in an age of liberation where moderation no longer matters. Not that it ever did, but now addictions are out in the open for all and sundry to see. Females like my pretty Tanya spread her legs not for a husband but a thick, buzzing stick in a collection of colors that drew her moan just as loudly as my little harem, now long gone, used up and turned to dust.

A part of me likes this new world, the power I've inadvertently collected in my absence, who I can become in its age of technology I've taken steps to understand. And I like the way the girl—*singular*—I choose to stalk teases and flirts and walks away from her dates and returns to her solo existence above the coffee shop with a secret smile on her face that no one is able to decode.

But I know. I watch her come over and over each night until the city disappears for me and I see only her.

Now, so close to Christmas, I know tonight she'll lie alone on her bed, and my time stalking her has come to a point of action. A call to it, like a siren's song.

Her dark hair flips over her shoulder as she watches me through almond eyes, dark and framed with the sort of thick, curled lashes I've always had a soft spot for. Not too made up; she doesn't need extra help to enhance her natural glow. Some angel bestowed that gift upon her long ago. From the way her eyes peer sexily at me through her lashes, she absolutely understands the effect she has on the male of her species. Possibly a few females, too.

Which is her M.O. To peer through those lashes, all wanton and ripe for juicing, right before she whispers *goodnight*. She'll stand and sashay to the stairs hidden away behind a coded lock where her long line of whimpering, salivating dates with their leaking, erect cocks can't follow.

But I can.

One of my favorite pastimes is picking locks. And the best of those are the ones that sit well above ground level, where the facade of safety withers with height.

Finding her in her bed will be fun. Also, the terror in her eye before I put my clawed hand to good use on her stunning behind. A guy has to have hobbies, right? I savor every single one of mine. And I've had an eon to cultivate enough fantasies to fill even this debauched world that runs on a ceaseless stream of instant gratification. But right now...

"I remember you said work was getting boring." Her first date hit all the right notes: what she did for employment without actually telling me where. Her interests, without being specific. The topping she hates on a pizza.

Graphic designer, loves movies but not what sort or which ones, and pineapple heated up sucks, especially next to cheese.

I have to admit, I sympathize with that last. After our first date I ordered my first pizza from a place a few doors down, perched on the rooftop opposite in my full form like a statuesque gargoyle and devoured the lot from my claws, licking each one clean as she worked herself into a frenzy on her bed, all alone.

But not without an audience of one with a back-drop of a starless night.

For the first time she seemed to sense an extra presence and walked afterwards on wobbly legs to the window, toying with the heavy, red drapes that hung like thickest velvet. Tanya stared out at the city moving sluggishly through the cold night when everyone should have been hurrying to warmer places. Then, without a glance in my direction, even when I let the pizza box flutter to the sidewalk below in the hope she'd glance up and see my monstrous form, she pulled the drapes together.

Almost all the way.

That invitation to draw closer is the one I took whether she wanted me to, or not. Because the slim line of muted light let me view the most tantalizing glimpse of curved, plump thighs just right to dig my claws into and split apart before I tasted her center.

She did the job for me, spreading her legs wide as I watched, her fingers digging into the oh so soft flesh, and worked her fingers–four of them, her hands were that small—into her sweetly scented pussy until she gushed with a cry.

Tanya fell asleep with her legs spread wide, her glistening fingers draped across her stomach, and her chest still rising and falling a little faster than normal.

I knew; I checked her regular breathing on both our dates. Which brings me back to the one that, by my count, should be almost over, if she holds to her usual course of action.

"Work is...slow." She sighs, her blouse lifting a little, gifting me the barest glimpse of a slice of her tender belly across the table. Of course, I've seen so much more. Still, the tease is so sweet. I salivate at her effort. "I want something more challenging than ad copy and social media posts. But it pays enough and so...that's what I do."

"Perhaps it's time for a change." I shrug, leaning back in my chair as the conversation in the cafe hit a lull point. This human form itches. My horns ache to burst through and my tail is jammed up my own ass. "People often have more than one occupation these days, it seems."

Tanya watches me with a crinkled brow. "You sound like an old man, yet you look too young for gray hairs."

"Appearances can be deceitful."

Her lips turn down, and her watchful eyes never leave me, much like the way I can't stop seeing her whether she's awake or asleep. "Why do you put it that way?"

"What way?" I toy with my cup, twirling it in quick circles without spilling a drop of the burnt milk and overcooked beans.

"Deceitful. That's not the phrase. Everything about you is..."

Slightly off.

She doesn't need to say it; we both follow her thoughts. And she's right in that gut instinct. If she's smart and varies her habits, it might save her one day.

But not from me.

I reach across the table and clasp her hand like the lovelorn fucker I most certainly am not.

Obssesser, not a lover. I mangle their phrases with pride.

Not a lover tonight, anyway. Right now, I have goals.

Tanya remains seated, though her smile strains. "I'm not very good at second dates."

I consider a moment, not letting her hands go and circle her wrist with my fingers. *Christ, she's small.* So much more fun to break later. "Not true. You just don't go on many."

Her hands leave mine with a sharp tug that only

frees her because I let go. From the way her eyes flare as she wraps her arms around herself, she knows it, too.

"Thank you for the coffee, Mister David."

Her eyes skate over me dismissively, but not before they narrow, taking in everything I want her to see and a few things I don't.

"Devlin." I supplied the fake name that appears to fit this form best, knowing she didn't really forget.

"Devlin. Of course," she murmurs.

And she turns, leaving me with a half drunk cappuccino and part of a shared date loaf she never touched.

I don't blame her. The damn stuff tastes like poison.

Her jeans fit perfectly to the curves of her ass as she sashays away without a single glance over her shoulder. There will be no invitation from her tonight, or any other night. Not for me, her date last week, the one tomorrow, or the night after that.

No one ever gets up those stairs or between her pretty legs.

No one ever tastes her, and it's such a loss.

One I intend to change tonight.

Being on my naughty list has perks. And some other things.

CHAPTER TWO

TANYA

I never let anyone have a second date, but Devlin is just too bad to be true. In a good way. The quiet type you just *know* had a filthy mind under all that studiousness. The casual, confident air, bored with the world, ready to let it burn from within.

He could be a hacker, a social justice vigilante, a lawyer pushing the envelope. I never did get the answer out of him, and it shits me. Most dates *blah blah blah* their way through their allocated hour, desperate to divulge every life secret like it will earn them extra time, though it never does.

No, Devlin remains a mystery in more than one sense. That part of his anonymity appeals to me, too.

Not that I'd ever tell him so, or that I expected

anything to come of our second date, not that I'm sure why I agreed to it. But then he had to go and prove I was right by ruining it, didn't he? With that line that said he stepped in too close.

No, correction. He already crossed that line. Gotten inside my personal life, even if just by a fraction, and that's close enough to slam the proverbial door on not-Devlin's face.

That was the whole reason for No. Second. Dates.

Ever.

Not that you go on many.

His words and mine mingle in my head while I stare at the blank wall inside my apartment that glows with pink and gold reflected neon light from the broken sign on the adult shop across the road. I'm damn glad that shop is there because I've got quite the collection from their shelves.

Serial dater I am. Second dater? Never. Not really. Not until him. And he proved my theory correct the first time around.

Glaring at the bare wall, pink neon flashing in my periphery, I flip the bird at Devlin's imaginary shade, hoping he's already left downstairs, rather than sit at the table pining over the horrendous food and worse coffee.

If my stellar personality isn't enough to put my dates off for round two, then the fare should be next in line for the red flag parade.

As I turn away, I swear a shadow flickers in the corner of my eye, one similar to a devil shape, horns, tail, a few extra bits even. But when I turn back to the wall all I'm faced with is the reflection of the jolly fat man waving his stiff arm at me from across the street.

"Wrong season, psycho," I mutter, unsure who I'm speaking to—the flat version of capitalism incarnate, or my own conscience personified.

"Is it?" The words float around me.

I swivel to the window that sits half open, and empty.

Definite psycho.

Myself, this time. Only me.

I walk to the window and start to close it, pausing with my fingers on the ledge when it's so close to completely shut. Frigid night air curls around my wrist in an elegant, if icy caress. I let the tendrils numb my skin for a second, staring out at where I swear my night stalker sat across from me, watching the week before.

Or maybe I imagined the whole thing, and I'm just a lonely woman who refuses to go on second dates because I'm too scared to see what happens after that.

Because I understand the pain of rejection. How much it fucking well hurts to be left alone while the person you thought you'd spend the rest of your natural life with wanders off with some other side piece you didn't realize was actually the main event and you...

Weren't.

A wretched sound that's halfway between a whimper and a snarl that resembles roadkill's final death rattle leaves my lips. I slam the window shut hard enough to rock the glass in its frame. The memory fragments my window with its force, a fine crack that starts at the base of the pane and works its way upward in a spiderweb of fine crevices.

I stare out at San Francisco's bay, the sliver of it I can see. My view is splintered by the fractured glass. For no stupid reason at all, my eyes well with tears, further obscuring the city's lights until yellow and pink neon blur together over the landscape of Christmas nothingness.

Damn Devlin and his stalking habits. Why couldn't he be the one who watched me last week? A real stalker would have followed me up the staircase.

But I live above a public coffeehouse that's busy well into the night. The noise and the constant presence keeps me sane because when it gets too quiet I can hear myself *think*. And that's when I get destructive. My thumb runs along the line of scars hidden under my long-sleeved top that runs to my wrist from my elbow beneath the material.

Even in summer, I keep the sleeves on. Good thing for me they never go out of fashion. I keep the material lighter in the warmer months. Anything to hide the shame of the fact I can't deal with the ache within that tells me I'm not worthy of being here, sharing the air with the other mortals who seem to thrive on existing in their pithy lives the same plane as me.

Working their jobs, managing relationships that stay together day after day after day.

I blink away my tears for a moment, long enough to see a couple, their arms interlocked between their coats, walk into the coffee shop below. I want to bang on the broken glass, scream at them not to go in. That the coffee and the cake and the company is terrible...

And then I remember it's just me that's terrible, and they're safe.

"Stop it, *stop it*," I mutter to my psycho self,

prying my eyes open to stare into the demonic ones on the other side of my window.

The slitted ones fixed right back on me through a face of horror and nightmares, all angles and horns and inhumane swirls that peer soul deep like they recognize me.

A scream builds in the base of my throat, scratching my insides to escape, but it...doesn't

Because if I lean a little closer, there are similarities. The monster staring in at me isn't the only one who has a moment of recognition, like he's meant to be here.

Those cheekbones I swore I could cut my fingers on when I sat at the small table across from him downstairs, twice. The dark as coal eyes that absorbed light, rather than reflected it. Those arrogant, arched lips I wanted to know what it felt like when they covered mine, pried me open and forced his tongue inside my mouth.

Muted my pleasured screams, because I knew he'd be that good.

Before he ruined it all by fessing up to being the perfect little stalker, and then not hauling his obsessive ass up the stairs behind me.

And now here he is, in the flesh, with a monster

suit on. Only, this monster is adhered to his skin, and it's not plastic, or prosthetics, or any other form of costume. No, I'm looking at the stuff of true nightmares. My fingers twitch on the windowsill where air slips in through the tiniest gap that's still open. I'm already hyperventilating with—*panic, need, insanity*—when Devlin-wearing-the-monster-suit raises a freaking *claw* that curves at the end like a proper talon, and taps on the broken glass like a perfect gentleman.

"Come on, Tanya," he purrs. "You know you want to let me in."

I stare back at him, my fingers lifting the sill before I've thought any further about this. Only half an inch, and my brain kicks into gear.

He's. A. Monster.

This is True Blood land and I'm no Sookie Stackhouse. Plus, I don't have anywhere near enough sharp implements in my apartment. The blade I use to mark myself up with is blunt, for fuck's sake, because I'm too scared of what I'd do if I used something sharp to flay myself. Hell, I remember from the series how hard it looked to get blood out of the floor.

Brain kicking into gear while I'm already admiring those horns that look at least nine inches

—how fucked up can a girl be?—I slam the window shut.

It doesn't make the noise it's supposed to, though *he* does.

"That hurt, Little One," he murmurs, those bottomless eyes swirling with emotion and—is that *need*? "I don't mind starting a list of my own." He extracts one of those claws and waves them at me, flesh morphing from hardened, dark whatever-he-is-covered-in back to his human pinkish form.

Humans really are like little goober pink worms.

The innocuous thought roils around my head while I gape at him. The window flies open—apparently pink skin means strength remains—and he steps through the open space like he walked in off the street, not the second story.

"Were you just walking on air?" I stare, and shut my mouth. "And close the window. It's fucking cold."

He smirks at me, sliding the single clawed hand into his pocket. "I knew you had a filthy mouth, Tanya. Goes with that filthy fucking cunt you play with every night."

It was him.

My heart rate picks up as he addresses the non-elephant in the room, because the obvious one is—well, okay. So, there's a few.

"What are you going to do if I scream bloody murder?" I ask, more curious than anything.

My suicidal tendencies kick in. Everyone else might have that fight, freeze or flight thing going on. I just want to talk to the monster who perches his perfect behind on the end of my bed.

He looks up at me, licking his lips and rubs the quilt with his hand—no claws in sight—in a soothing motion. "Come sit down, Tanya," he suggests.

"Murder," I remind him, pointedly.

"Ah. That."

"Yes, th—"

His claw closes around my throat from behind, the long fingers wrapping all the way to restrict my airflow, though they're long enough to creep up my jaw and push my head back.

"I could snap your neck, but I like my victims alive and kicking when I play with them," he says in that same conversational tone he used downstairs when he dropped his other bomb.

"Oh," I wheeze and tap the back of his claw. "Ai-ai— pl–zz?" I raise an eyebrow as my lungs threaten to burst.

He frowns at me. "Your lung capacity is fucking terrible."

The claw releases my throat. I bend over at the waist, sucking in air and realize it's probably the worst position for it. I stay bent over anyway, reasoning it's the closest place to the floor if I'm going to pass out. The way tiny pinprick glittery dots swim across my vision, it's a fifty-fifty thing.

"Are we good on the screaming position, now?" Devlin crouches at my side, peering up into my face. Gentle hands push my hair back when I don't respond, bar a few desperate gasps.

I hold up a hand, still attempting to fill that shit-house lung capacity we discussed a moment before. "Yeah, we're good. Why are you—" I cough, and he rubs my back in a surprisingly tender motion, leading me back to my bed.

"It's a small room, isn't it? Thank you for leaving the drapes open for me."

I find myself planted ass first on my bed, his hands trailing up and down my back. His touch is soothing, and I lean into the monster on my bed.

"Ah, you're welcome?" I blink, recalling his comment from before. I should be embarrassed. I should be...something, but all I feel is...wanted.

Yeah, I'm beyond fucked up. Deal.

"Better," he murmurs approvingly.

Some of the hardness changes his face, and I half reach up before I hesitate, then just go for it.

"Can I see them? Please?"

His eyes widen for a fraction of a second before a slow hiss leaves his lips. "You like this form, Tanya?"

Devlin's body literally ripples before me. Shoulders, stomach, face. It all changes, his skin darkening and toughening into a different sort of all-over covering, somewhere between a harder form of flesh. It's almost stone, or bark, but not quite. My mind can't make sense of what I'm seeing. His jawline becomes fixed, the lines around his ears and cheeks solidifying.

And those horns. Oh, sweet baby monsterlings, those *horns.*

I had no idea that was even a fetish until this moment.

"So beautiful." My whisper hangs between us as he watches me through hooded eyes, the slits tracking every breath that feels more like a pant at this point.

"You're not at all what I expected."

His confession stops my reaching hands.

"What?" I blink at him. "Is that bad? And, can I still touch? Please," I throw in some manners belatedly, hoping it might get me somewhere.

His laugh is a deep rumble that fills the room, curling around me. "Hold that thought."

The light flickers off, shrouding us in darkness before I realize there is no us, and I perch on my bed alone.

No, not alone. Like before when he suddenly appeared behind me, he's just moved to—

Those razor edged claws slide around my waist, the tips shredding my shirt, biting into my stomach. *No blunt edges served here.*

"I have a deal for you, Tanya. If you agree, you can play with the horns for as long as you like."

My breath hitches. "And if I don't agree?"

His soft, deep laugh fills my room as he methodically ruins my shirt, working his way along my stomach.

CHAPTER THREE

DEVLIN

I never offer deals. Nor, with Tanya, do I have a clue what I'm doing. My mouth seems intent on running away with itself tonight, much as my hands strip her bare, inch by torturous inch. Sometimes my claws slash lightly at her flesh, scoring and marking her, though she does little more than shiver in my arms with each harsh touch.

It isn't until I peel back her top that covers her body from my view, leaving her in only her lacy bra that doesn't hide her distended nipples, peaked and budded tight, or the scars that cover her wrist to elbow, that I understand.

My claws freeze over the damaged skin, and a low growl rips through my chest.

"What is it?" She frowns, tilting her head back to look up at me. "I wear a bra. It's a common thing. I don't know how long you watched me for, or how many women you've been with—"

Snapping my teeth in her ear, I flip her over onto her back, forcing a knee roughly between her thighs to spread her legs. My claws pull her arms over her head as I haul her body across the width of the bed until her head almost hangs over one end, her hair trailing the floor, our feet dangling off the other side.

Her wrists I clasp in my claws, but her scars I trace with my very human thumb, stroking the ruined skin where she's cut into herself a hundred times or more. I can see where she started light, even a few frenzied patches. Then the times she's gone harder, hacking at herself as though trying to cut some part of herself away.

"What's this?" I growl, arching over her until our noses touch, and glare into her eyes.

To her credit, she doesn't cry or scream or flinch away. I've had human males piss themselves in terror at less from me, but she watches my eyes with a sort of detachment I instantly hate.

A quick shake of my hand on her wrists brings

her back to me. "Answer me," I bark. "Or the horns go, Little One."

A moment of silence. Then—

"I didn't want to feel anymore," she confesses, her lips tight.

"Bullshit. Don't lie to me, Tanya," I warn her. Two dates in we might be, but I've watched her for far longer, know her intimate habits. Or at least, I thought I did.

Now...I breathe hard against her cheeks, scant inches from doing something I can't control to the obsession in my arms. Because I *didn't know she hurt.*

And I wasn't here to hold her, make it go away.

"I wanted out. But I was too scared to do anything..." Her gaze slides sideways.

My patience ends. "Stop it," I snap. "Feed the bullshit to someone else. I'm the monster in your motherfucking bed. Give me the truth, or I'll rip it from your flesh myself."

Her eyes gloss with a sheen of tears. Horror swamps me that I've terrified her that much.

She's not the one.

I'd hoped...

After removing myself from the world for so long I wanted to find just one woman to spend my next waking years with. She'd still be mortal, and I'd still outlive her, but I wanted to have someone to love and care for. Protect. Taunt and tease and fucking well *date*.

Tanya isn't the only one who never makes it to a second date. I hoped with her I could change that, maybe for both of us. It looks like maybe I hoped wrong.

"I'm sorry, Little One. I didn't mean to–"

"I'd love it if you would hurt me," she blurts.

I freeze. Every single part of me locks painfully tight. My head tilts to one side as my heart, the organ I thought long dead, hammers in my chest.

Now there's a deal I can take.

"And why would I do that?" I play the uninterested Krampus, scratching my claws lightly along the edges of her scars where I know she'll be sensitive. She's not my first cutter, but by all the dark Christmas nights out there, I hope she's my only for this century.

"Because your version of sex isn't vanilla either, demon boy," she taunts in a cracked whisper, those tears still glossing her eyes, though her fears are yet to break their banks.

My breath comes short as she nails me in an instant.

"Let's talk about that demon problem of yours." I

run my nose along her cheek, inhaling her sweet, heady scent. *No, I'm not wrong.* "I'm a Krampus, Tanya. Do you know what that is?" She shakes her head. I tsk, letting my forked tongue flicker between my lips, displaying the wares. Her soft gasp hardens me. "It means I'm the opposite of all things the big red man does at this time of the year. He's my brother, the elder by one minute. He got the responsibilities, while I received other...gifts."

"Oh." Her arms relax as I stroke her, her body stretching out as I settle my weight over her softer form. I let my hips contact her, grinding our bodies together. Those pretty eyes fly wide. "*Oh–*"

"I like midnight screams." I lick the corner of her lips. "I like ropes and chains." Tasting her throat is my new favorite addiction. "And I love to find out how many stripes it takes to warm your pale flesh with my hand and other...instruments." I smirk when her eyes cloud with a stunning combination of confusion and lust. "Spanking, Little One. I have a spanking fetish. I'm not above using funishments as a form of motivation. Maybe I'll edge you into next week. Maybe I'll let you cum all over my tail." I flick the thick muscle around one of her legs and jerk her wide open.

Her fingers flex. "Can I touch you?' she begs.

She's not screaming, yet.

For all the wrong reasons.

"Fuck me, that's a pretty sight. I thought you'd be a brat through and through."

"I mean, I can be that, too. But...not right now." Her liquid gaze travels up, but she hesitates. "I don't want to offend you, or anything."

My laughter fills her room. "There's a monster pinning you to your bed, has ruined your clothes. I've broken into your home, threatened you, and you're worried about *offending me*?" I stare down at her.

"Horns, and I want to know how you kiss," she whispers back.

Damn, I want those things now, too.

"Deal," I remind her.

Tanya sighs and wiggles torturously. Okay, so maybe laying my weight over her was not the smartest idea ever. "Okay, what's the deal?"

"Four days. Four dates. At night. This form. Human, during the day. If you can put up with me for that period, you're mine. If you can't, you're free."

Christmas night is my deadline. It's always been a sore spot so I may as well go with it.

She frowns at me. "That's a stupid deal."

I raise my eyebrows at her. "Let's hear yours, then."

Her mouth opens and closes, then opens again. "You come to my room each night after I finish work. We screw until Christmas. *Maybe* New Year's if the sex is really excellent and you don't puff into Krampus ash on the twenty-fifth. Then, you go your way and I..." She shrugs underneath me.

It's not really so different from what I just suggested. But still, it's missing some of the finer points I require. Like keeping her.

"You, what? Return to the shitty life you've been living for the past however long?" I lick the corner of her mouth, savoring her taste. "No."

"Fine. Then I guess we agree to not deal."

"I don't think that's how the line goes."

"Whatever, demon."

There's the brat I knew was in there.

She says it just to piss me off. I know that.

"Fine, Little One. Last chance. We fuck around until Christmas. A few days. Tell me it's the best sex you've ever had or not. I don't care." *Lie.* "But at the end, if you know you can't live without the horns and monster in your life, you're mine. For the rest of this life. If I can't give you all the orgasms you ever need in the next days, if you're not as addicted to me as I am to you, then I'll walk away and never watch you ever again."

She freezes. "You'd never come back. Like, ever?"

"Never." I watch her face carefully.

"Oh." She shuts down.

I risk releasing one of her wrists to catch her jaw when her gaze skates away from me. *You don't get to escape from me. Not like that. Not again.* My little Tanya has a habit of retreating inward when she can't deal with what's happening around her. Maybe I overwhelm her. Maybe that last deal is too much. Maybe I fucked up and lost her. I still have no idea.

But damn if I don't want to steal at least one kiss before she kicks me out like a bad Krampus, tail tucked between my legs.

My other hand strokes her scars absently as I feather her jaw with my other hand, forcing her gaze back to mine. "What do you say, Little One? Will you risk my deal?"

Her breath stalls as she looks up at me. No, not at me. Past me.

"Which one lets me touch the horns?"

CHAPTER FOUR

TANYA

I'm insane. I know that as Devlin releases my hands, breath whooshing from his enormous chest cavity. Letting my needs guide me, I coast my fingers along the thickened flesh on his face, over his solid, rough cheekbones, and higher, until my hands curve around his horns.

Or they try to. Because those suckers are thick. A low groan leaves Devlin's mouth, his body shifting against mine. It isn't until I glance back at his face, my attention lost on the ridges and whorls decorating the stunning horns that rear back like weapons in their own right, that I register what that groan means.

His attention is locked on me, and the third horn

between his legs feels as thick as the ones on his head as his bulge grinds into my covered pussy.

"Oh, wow," I whisper. "I didn't know–"

HIs next sound is less of a groan and more of a warning growl before his mouth crashes over mine, his thick, split tongue delving deep. My answering whimper as he stuffs my throat with his tongue is a muted sound, though an approving echo rumbles from his chest as his body weight sinks over me.

There's a Krampus in my bed, and I don't want him to leave.

After all the online trawling for relationships that just won't work, the two *years* of first dates that won't quit on me, I finally feel as though I've hit the end of a long night, and found rising dawn. A stupid sentiment, because the dark fire wreathing Devlin's eyes is nothing like the sun blazing through my windows. I've trialed them all: the banker, the security guard. The hairdresser, the gym buff. None of them were remotely interested in anything but themselves.

Until Devlin.

If Christmas morning smells like fresh snow and cranberry tea, then my Krampus tastes like elicit midnight kisses beneath a clear, cold sky, burnt cinnamon quills, and mulled wine.

His body ripples between his human and monster form, as though he can't decide who he wants to be in this moment. Not that I can blame him; if I had a choice on it, I'm not sure, either. The man who sat across from me downstairs and watched me with those coal dark eyes that gave away nothing yet absorbed everything, the man with the arrogant lips that didn't *quite* curl up into a smirk, though the corners hinted at hidden knowledge. I understand that persona is just a cover for the monster above me, and I want them both. I understand why I couldn't read him properly, because he wasn't real. Or, at least, he wasn't all of the real Devlin.

Now, I know what he knows. I want what he wants.

Devlin grinds his hips into me, his bulge thickening impossibly. Even in this form, he'll ruin me, tear me apart. But then, I did just beg him for pain from those large, roughened hands tipped with claws that systematically shredded my top, leaving me bare and exposed before him. Claws that left fine marks on my skin like he knows just how to control himself, but can't help tracing red lines over my pale flesh anyway.

And I love it. Everything he does. My body, every

part of me that resides deeper than my bones, aches for what he might gift me.

Apparently I'm particularly reckless tonight.

"I can control it, Tanya," he murmurs, breaking the kiss long enough to trail that sexy as all get out tongue across my bottom lip twice in a move so possessive I'm shocked I don't melt into my quilt covers on the spot. "If I hurt you, it's by design."

That should not be so hot.

"You're a not-tame monster with a conscience?" I raise an eyebrow, undulating my hips to tease us both, but mainly because the movement hits the spot right *there—*

Devlin jerks back like I've slapped him. "Uh uh. No topping from the bottom, Little One," he utters, squeezing my arms harder than before.

A zing of pleasure at his rough handling replaces the disappointment of not being able to sneak a tiny orgasm past him.

"But you said endless pleasure, or something like that." I ignore him, or pretend to, studying the ceiling.

Don't watch the sexy monster slithering over your body. Don't look at the horns. Don't look—

Will he moan if I lick them?

"Keep your filthy thoughts in your head until

we've finished negotiating, Tanya." Devlin rises over me, his elliptical pupils wild and obsessive.

We've scooted well past the realm of possession by now. This, whatever the hell this is, we've hit something I don't understand, but I want to be a part of it anyway.

"Did I say that out loud?" My mouth stretches in a saccharine smile, fake but not, dripping in the sort of sweet treat I instinctively know he can't refuse.

This is why no one ever got a second date, except for him. Because no one ever *got me*. No one had that underlying darkness that matches mine.

It's not that I want to tame the monster under my bed; I want a monster in my bed to tame *me*.

I knew someone watched me that night. The drapes I left ajar were for voyeuristic reciprocal pleasure alike. I *knew* someone was out there, and I hoped it was him.

Now I know, just as I know I'll take his stupid deal because that's part of this spiral, isn't it? Let him take control, see how far we can fly together, his hand collaring my neck, before he laughs in my face and sets me plummeting in freefall.

I'll take his deal. He'll have to work it out of me, because he's right about one thing.

I am a brat.

CHAPTER FIVE

DEVLIN

What the hell am I doing handing out deals with this girl who has fast become my obsession, and tasting the secret places of her warm, wet mouth? That last quite literally is a joy as she writhes beneath me, her slight body supple with all the right curves.

I need to earn more of those delicious sounds she makes when I stroke my tongue along hers with that dual touch she can't get anywhere else. Sure, I've seen these humans leave their tattoo parlors with their cut tongues, but theirs can't divide the length mine can, can't bring her the sort of pleasure when I pierce her pussy with the twin lengths and fuck her like I've got two cocks, teasing her swollen folds.

When I woke and came to this place months ago, I found her as though she called me across oceans, drawing me to her. Setting up a base nearby I made sure I learned everything about this world, all its kinks and delights, what I wanted from it, what she needs most. I learned her dating habits as I taught myself the economics of this place, what she would need from a mate to protect her.

What she needs at a flesh deep level night after night.

Her guttural moan undoes me as she seems to catch on to my plan for the night, her short, blunt nails digging into my shoulders. My shirt pulls tight.

"Get this off," she demands, but I push her back.

"Agree to my terms." I snap my teeth at her throat, and she freezes. A slow smile curves my lips. "Did you think me a monster you could tame, push under your bed like your box of toys and drag out whenever you wanted to play on your schedule?"

"What, be yours?" Her gaze slides from my mouth to my eyes, and holds there, a flicker of— *something*—behind them.

I trail a claw down her waist and shred the rest of her clothing with a flick, leaving her bare—well, bare, if rags don't count—beneath me. "You're a pretty distraction, but that mouth of yours has other uses. Agree, or you'll find out how brutal I can be."

Her lashes fly wide, and I swear she fucking *glows*.

Like a dark candle in the center of a seance, its flame flaring brightest.

"Yes, please," she begs, and bites her lip. Her brow dips as she watches me and something about her glow...dims.

I fucking hate it. "What?" I snap, closing my claws around her waist, digging the points in until she cries out. "Don't you hide from me," I warn her.

Those pretty eyes flare wide again, and my hands relax.

"No, don't stop," she whispers, smiling when I squeeze her again. Breath leaves her lips on a strangled sound I know she tries to hide, but she'll learn she doesn't have to, not with me.

"Tell me, Little One. I have less patience than usual. Especially in this form." I let my darker side take true form, tearing the clothing I donned for her, ripping the seams out of my pants and the back of my shirt until they hang off me in ragged panels. My thick thighs press her legs wider, my cock seeking her heat.

One word is all I need, and I'll stretch her wider than she's ever known, brand her as my own. I might have lied about the patience factor, but then, I lie about a lot of things.

Hey, I'm not the jolly brother, alright? Lies, deceit, darkness…that's my domain. And this girl was made for me, predestined in some other age. I know now I've been waiting for her, marking time for centuries, learning everything I can about human women in order to please her.

I need her cries like I need blood ricocheting around my body. Her breath of my chest as she traces over the swirls on my pecs, scratches the hardened flesh with her nails until I grind against her again and leave her eyes rolling in her head with pleasure, and we haven't. Even. Fucking. Started.

Her smile becomes more *her* as she coasts her gaze back to meet mine. Unafraid, open and accepting.

The only screams I draw from her will be ones of pure pleasure. Or pain. Whatever she begs for most.

Fine hands tug at my rags. "At least now we match."

The tip of her pink tongue sweeps across her bottom lip, and I'm done.

Deal or no deal, I'm hers.

CHAPTER SIX

TANYA

I know the moment I get exactly what I want from the monster in my bed. Wiggling my hips, I tempt him with everything those soul dark eyes desire as I lift one hand and glide it over his horns.

Devlin's control snaps.

His hips surge forward as he fills me in one thrust. Pain and pleasure melds, my world fuzzying —I'm not sure that's a word but it fits for the visual white noise that crowds my existence at the edges with snow—as I drop back, still clinging to one horn like my life depends on that death grip.

The crazed lust in his eyes should terrify me. *This is the moment I die, impaled on a monster cock* in a cheap apartment above a coffee shop where everyone hates the food and the burned, roasted beans.

I open my mouth to provide the scream he seems to want, but the thick tongue that matches his fat cock fills me until all that comes out is a muddled noise that could be mistaken for begging.

Life, air, *more.*

I don't know who I am, but if this is how my existence ends, I'm here for the whole ride.

Devlin pumps his hips deliberately, driving that thick third horn deep. My scream bubbles along my throat and like before he swallows my sacrificial sound on the altar of my rumpled bed.

I want to roll my hips up to meet him, but I'm lost in an overwhelm of sensation, frozen in place. Breaths come short, and from the way he holds me, fierce and unyielding, I'm not alone in my captive state.

Forcing my hands to glide along his shoulders, I let my eyes shutter for a moment, and feel. *Everything.* The heat of him, melting into me. The heavy weight of him where he sinks into my hips and retreats to slide back again. The pain/pleasure split inside me aided by my copious slick because I'm a whore for the monster I've invited into my bed.

And then my hands take a little tour of their

own, exploring his jawline, running through his hair. My thumb runs across the base of his horn, and he *shudders*.

"Does my monster like that?" I tease, managing to force the words in a thin whisper from my throat when he gives me a chance at air.

"Your monster?" he rasps, his eyes blackening out in totality. "Does that make you my human? My little pretty treat?"

"Yes," I whisper back.

"Mine?" he asks wonderingly.

I nod and he *moves*.

Devlin's hips almost blur as he rails my lower body as he promised, claws digging into my softer flesh like I begged him for the pain. My legs wind around him as far as I can, though his strong, muscular thighs keep me spread wide apart. And I *drip*. My orgasm builds fast where his body pounds into mine, slapping my clit on repeat until I scream into his shoulder, biting down with the force of my bliss.

His roar reverberates next to my ear, the sound deafening as he fills me, searing my insides. After Devlin, I know I'll never be the same. It doesn't take a genius to know he shouldn't have fit and probably tore me. But right now I'm floating on the sort of euphoric afterglow that consumes me.

I never want to come down.

"Fuck, you're incredible." His kiss between strained breaths is rough, the bruising variety. He utters the hollowest laugh. "You know what you've done, Tanya?"

"What?" My body comes back to me, aching and fluttering around him in all the right/wrong places.

His dark laugh in my ear as he thickens inside me again sends every nerve ending screaming. "You just reduced my deal offer to two days. I need an answer now, Little One. I need to know if I'm your forever. Because I'm not sure if I can take a no on not taking you on as mine."

"I don't think I'm supposed to agree to anything in this state—" I start, but then he moves again, and my ability to talk ceases altogether.

And all I see is the Krampus undulating above me, his lips curled back in an inhumane snarl as he works my body over like it's an instrument designed just for him. My scream hovers at the back of my throat, but his claw clamps down around my airway, closing off what I need. I grip his wrist, or try to, but he's that much bigger than me in this form. For the first time I realize how frail, how fragile I am next to him.

His other claw drags down to my hip, the sharp tips curving around to pierce my skin as his tongue flickers out to taste my breathless cries. It's too much to take. His thrusts grow wild, claiming. My body tightens as he delivers exactly what he promised: insane pleasure that fractures my mind.

I scream silently, my open mouth an invitation for his split tongue to enter as I flood his cock with my bliss, mixing our fluids together. This time, the world doesn't turn fuzzy at the edges with white noise.

This time, the world grays out altogether, with him my anchor to it. And then even he fades on a bed of endless pleasure that runs on and on as I fall suspended by his claws.

Sunlight filters through my apartment. Gone are the flickering yellow and pink neon reflections with the night, the chatter from the shop below as the city begins to wake with the fresh sunlight. I stretch on the fresh sheets, naked beneath the crisp cotton. Warmth slants across my skin that aches in places it shouldn't. I frown, running my hands over my skin and wince, looking down.

My stomach and hips are covered in scratches. Fine, thin scratches, made by—

The night floods back to me, along with every ache, but my bed is only occupied by a single body.

My Krampus has left me with the sun, though my cracked window sits ajar. My body is clean, though between my legs is swollen, though far from the sustained damage is expected. I clutch my pillow, one hand trailing to my hip where I expected my body to be as shredded as my clothes.

My clothes.

I roll to the side of my bed, ignoring my body's protests at the movement, and hang my head over the edge. Not a single skerick of my destroyed clothing lies on the floor. Instead, I spot a black, sparkling dress that hangs over my single worn chintz I use as a reading seat when the mood hits.

My phone buzzes, jerking me out of my Krampus sex-induced haze. Smiling, I pick up the device, all too ready to continue our banter from last night. My thighs twinge a little as I stretch, but that's all. My head tells me my body should hurt more as I turn my phone over, and open the screen.

And frown.

. . .

> Samson: Ditch the boss man. He's not good for you.

> Samson: I'll take you somewhere classy tonight.

I groan and roll back onto my bed, prepared to toss my phone out the window. *Not this dickhead again.* Samson was an early date, over a year ago. Shy of blocking him, which I grow closer to on a daily basis, I regret ever having teased him with sexting before we actually caught up in person.

Because he's another let-down-date who simply never measured up in person. A beefy guy who ran security jobs, I thought he might be interesting. Yeah, interested about himself. That was where the buck stopped. He's far from the sort of lover I seek. Nothing like my monster who, though possessive and maybe a little obsessed, is a ridiculously generous lover.

Sighing, I consider not replying, but if I don't cut this conversation off now, Samson will rant on and on, and my mental health will plummet.

. . .

Tanya: I don't do second dates.
Sorry.

That last is a lie, but it seems to suit the situation. Maybe it will even placate him. Tossing my phone onto my pillow, I turn back to survey Devlin's offering. The dress. Third date.

The concept isn't half as terrifying as perhaps it should be.

Rolling my lip inward, I pad naked to the chair and pick up the dress. No note accompanies it, but it's a stunning confection of velvet stripes and black sequins. Not something I ever thought should go together but in this case, they do.

Apparently, without agreeing to his deal, I have a third date with Devlin.

The worst part is, I don't even mind that much. I place the dress back on the chair, and head to my cupboard to get ready for work, unwilling to wash the scent of him from my body.

Tonight can't come fast enough.

CHAPTER SEVEN

DEVLIN

I don't tackle the stairs. She might want me to knock on that door or come in through the window like last night, but Tanya is going to have to put on her big girl panties because we are actually going to leave the building.

Taking a seat at the same table I met her at last night before she tried to blow me off, I flick open my cuffs and roll my sleeves back, wondering how many shots of shithouse coffee I'll have to endure before she'll grace me with her presence.

Spoilers: she turns up when I'm rolling the second cuff.

I don't rise, continuing my work, methodical as always. Except for last night when I fucked us both into her bed until the damn thing threatened to collapse beneath us and I was surprised they didn't shut the cafe early.

Or maybe they did. I wouldn't have a clue because it was well after midnight when I slipped back out the window into the icy night air after washing her and cleaning her room. I refused to leave the woman I claimed until I was satisfied she was healing, inside and out, licking every inch of her I damaged until the cuts closed under the happy properties of my saliva.

A trait I learned today is often attributed in modern folklore to vampires but is in fact one of my own little tricks.

Usually after an event like last night I'd give a girl a break for a year and move onto the next house in the row. But for me there won't ever be a next house, and unknown to Tanya, I won't be moving on, ever. She's stuck with me whether she likes it or not. I'll be as persuasive as I need but at the end of the season I have a nice cave well away from humanity and I'm not above a little kidnapping job that will last the rest of her natural life.

There. That only sounds a little cute/creepy now, doesn't it?

Only if she doesn't agree to my terms, of course. And something tells me that she will.

"Are you ready?" I finally look up at her, having creased the last fold on my shirt and fuck me if I didn't pick the right dress for her from the shop I stole it from down the lane from her apartment less than eighteen hours ago.

Add kleptomaniac to my monthly sins quota.

Tanya looks way too edible in the black striped, glittery short gown that bares her legs. She's paired the very much not winter-proofed dress with thigh high velvet boots and a thick, fluffy black coat that looks stunning. Something I could burrow into, shred and unwrap her like she's my personal Christmas gift.

I've never been much into presents, but this year, she's mine.

"Ready for...?" Tanya licks at the red gloss she's coated her lips with, seems to remember it's there, and stops.

"Our date." I rise smoothly, sliding my arms into my jacket I draped over the back of my chair when I arrived and hold out my hand, claw free and palm up. "You look delicious."

"I don't think you're supposed to say that," she murmurs, her cheeks two bright, even spots of color as the man at the table next to us glances up and checks her out.

One look from me, and his attention returns to his own date, his arms stiff on his table.

I lean into her, tucking her hair behind her ear. "I can say whatever the fuck I want around these boring people with their basic little lives. Did you enjoy creaming all over my cock last night, Little One?"

She giggles softly, leaning into me. "Yes," she whispers back.

"Good girl," I praise her, my heart ramping up when she glows back at me. My hand folds around hers, and I haul her out of the cafe, dropping more than enough coinage on the table to cover my costs. "Come on."

"Where are we going?" She trots behind me as I head out the door, along the street and take a sharp corner down a narrow lane. "Devlin?" A hesitant note enters her voice.

I stop on the spot and turn to her, letting my claws curve around her hand, and cup her cheek. "Nothing and no one can hurt you while I'm here, you beautiful creature. Do you understand that? Nothing." I searched her face, needing to gain her confession. I know she hasn't agreed to my deal, either of them, but this is more important.

She nods, and it's not perfunctory. "I know."

"Good." I lean closer and press a chaste kiss to the corner of her mouth. "I want to take you somewhere I found when I woke and discovered what the world was like."

"How long did you sleep?" She skips to catch up, walking at my side and slinks under my arm, tucking her way against my ribs.

I laugh softly, hauling her closer, wrapping her in tight. It's what she seems to need, and I have no objection in providing her with that right now. She'll need her courage and no small amount of strength for what comes after.

"Many hundreds of years. The world is different. People aren't. They think this time is faster but they're all the same. Some processes are different. Superstitions are replaced with technology." I tap the phone tucked into her pocket that mirrors the one in mine. "Instant gratification is the trend over loyalty. Every generation has its whores for power. People haven't changed that much." I shrug as I turn into a black doorway that's as unmarked as any other we've passed and rap my knuckles sharply on its matte black surface.

"Where are we?" Tanya asks nervously.

I smile and press my lips to the top of her head, inhaling the scent of night jasmine that wafts around her in a heady halo. "You'll see. Trust me?"

"Of course."

That she answers without hesitation leaves me high with desire. Squeezing her fingers, I pull her in tighter, dragging my chin across her cheek to urge her head to tip back and claim her mouth in a rough kiss. Her lips part beneath my onslaught. When I pull back her eyes are half lidded with need, and the door stands open. A heavyset doorman in a close fitting suit stands off to one side, waiting in the cloak of the shadows, his face out of sight and doesn't disturb us until our display ends.

"Mister Myra," Beau murmurs, motioning us inside. I slide her jacket off and mine and pass them to him. I nod to my man who disappears deeper into the darkness as if by magic, though he only takes our things to the cloakroom I insisted on by the door.

"Mrya?" Tanya murmurs with a frown.

I cast her an amused glance. "Did you think St. Nick didn't have a family name?"

Her eyes widen as she pulls her hand back a fraction. I refuse to let her go, dragging her inside the building as Beau shuts the door discreetly behind us, locking it again and resumes his night's post in the dark.

Tanya's startled gasp leaves me half hard. I lead her through a rabbit warren of twists and turns in the darkness designed to disorient, and push open an invisible side door I rearranged earlier.

"Have you been to a sex club before, Tanya?" I ask, pulling her inside and shutting the door before pushing her back against it and palming the lock.

"N-no."

"Mmm. They work fairly simply. Members have their rules to play by. No drugs or alcohol while playing, no permanent damage. Rooms are booked for an elected purpose or time period. A safe word is agreed upon. The couple or group—" I let the word hang for a moment to allow her mind to wander, "— might negotiate the terms of the night's activities. Does that sound fair?"

"About as fair as your deal."

"Have you played before?"

"No." Her body softens as I lean into her. "But I've always wanted to."

"Good. If you had to pick a safe word, something you won't say by accident tonight, what would it be?"

"Hamster."

I laugh out loud. "Damn, girl. You'll be the death of me."

Her hands rise to find my face in the all-encompassing shadow, my features still human. I let her fingertips depress into my skin and she draws me down to her, using the single point of contact as a frame of reference.

"If I use that word tonight, will you listen?"

"Will you trust me to hear you?" I whisper back, licking the shell of her ear.

"After last night?" she considers. "Not in the least."

I laugh again. "You're perfect. Any other night I'd ignore it. Here, I'll play by the rules."

"What's different about here?" I read the curiosity in her tone.

"I own the place."

My mouth finds hers in a slow, exploratory kiss. She opens for me with the slightest flick of my tongue, letting me delve inside to taste her. The blacked out room removes one sense, heightening the others. I spent years in total darkness and am intimately acquainted with its properties.

Letting my hands wander over her body as I kiss her senseless against the door, still in my human form, her soft moans and shattered breaths tell me this is something she has never experienced before, but that being here both unnerves and excites her.

"This way." I back up, holding only her fingertips, and break contact with her everywhere else.

"Dev–" she whispers, grabbing for my fingers as I slip away into the darkness, turning around her.

The room is huge, the size of a small auditorium. Usually I have furniture set around the room for displays, but all that's been pushed aside for tonight. I left the stairs open that lead to my current home here. If she heads up there, I swear I'll lock her away for her version of an eternity and never let her free.

But that's a fantasy for another night.

Right now I wander behind her, listening for her increasingly frantic breaths, her heels clipping an erratic staccato against the floor. Her panic increases as she turns herself around completely, heads off in the wrong direction, and stops.

"Dev," she calls, pleading already.

I strip off my shirt and pants, kicking off my shoes in silence, and place everything against the wall where we came in. She's stopped, her panic rising though her senses have kicked in.

"Good girl," I murmur as I stride back toward her, my tail lashing out to secure both her wrists and pull them aside before my claws are on her. My mouth follows, sucking and nipping at her sensitive skin.

Sharp cries rip from her, the mewling noises dying a fast death in the empty, sound proofed room. I closed the club for tonight. Beau, my doorman, is the only other person in the building, and he's only there in case we need anything for the next two hours on extra pay. After that, he's free to head home. Not that he'll be able to hear us unless I call him, and my phone is currently parked with my clothes well away from us.

Speaking of...

"You're overdressed." I trail my claws along her lips. "Lick." I pace the sharpened tips on her tongue and wait.

She licks, hesitant, and I can fucking well *smell* her need as she nearly comes for me on the spot.

"Please, Dev," she gasps, pushing her body up against mine.

"I thought we had this little talk about topping from the bottom," I chastise her. My tail yanks her hands above her head as I slash the dress from her body, running my palm over her flesh to rub the ruined cloth away and finding no undergarments beneath. "Dirty little slut," I mutter approvingly.

"Dress like this for every date and we will get along just fine."

"Do I get to pick the next date?" she gasps as I catch her nipple between two claw tips and roll it delicately without hurting her.

Tiny whimpers fall from her lips as she tries so damn hard to hold still. It's the most beautiful thing I've ever felt. "What did you have in mind?"

"I— oh, fuck," she moans as I slide my claws between her thighs and collect her juices, tracing around her swollen cunt lips. "I want to do something not sex based."

I freeze. "Is this something you don't enjoy?" I tap her dripping slit until my hand is coated in her juices making a liar out of the writhing girl in my grip. "Tell me," I demand.

"No, I just— I want to know we have more in common than fucking." She screams as I retract my claws and push three fingers knuckle deep inside her.

"More than begging me to come? More than giving you all the pleasure you could ever need?" I snarl as her knees shake and her pussy flutters around my fingers. Just as the first contraction hits, I yank my hand free of her cunt's tight grip and spank her pussy with a resounding slap that echoes around the empty room even though it shouldn't be able to with its muted properties.

Tanya cries over the ruined orgasm, her knees giving out as she collapses but my tail keeps her suspended. Just to be crueler, I lift her higher so if she doesn't stay on her toes, her shoulders take all her weight. Not that it matters to me, her body mass barely registers.

My chest heaves nonetheless, rage ripping through me.

"Are you always this harsh?" she sobs, hanging from my bonds, her feet scrabbling tiredly at the floor, and we've only just started.

I grip her face in my human hand, squeezing tight enough to bruise her. More whimpers fall from her lips, a beautiful sound. "I thrive on your tears. Your pain, Little One. When you cry I want to pummel that tight cunt and stretch you until your mind remembers only me. I want to erase those dates you went on, remove those memories from your mind. No one else touches you. They don't look at you. Only I taste you." I run my tongue along her bottom lip softly, teasing her with sweetness until she opens to me, and I kiss her gently.

"Possessive little Krampus aren't you," she purrs.

One hand cups between her thighs to find her

gushing fresh and hot. "Fuck, you like it." I pull back, amazed. She should be screaming and thrashing in my bonds. I expected to fuck her into submission again and again, reprogram and break her mind, turn her into what I need her to be. But Tanya...she's here for me as I am, ready now. "You're too perfect." I squeeze her mound until she moans, stretching up on her tip toes for balance, and grinds her pussy into my palm.

"I want a date that's not sex," she says clearly. "I don't care how much you punish me for it."

I consider her. "Your idea of punishment and mine might differ," I say mildly.

"Picnic. In the park."

I trace a finger along her ass crack to find her back hole and trace her fluids around the nerve endings there to tease her. "You are truly diabolical. Can I kiss you?"

"If it's romantic."

"When would this date take place?"

"Tomorrow. The day before Christmas."

"Deal." I close her off before she can run on any longer. "But tonight, you're mine."

And tomorrow, you'll limp through the entirety of your date.

CHAPTER EIGHT

TANYA

D evlin finally gets his deal. At least, part of one. Somehow, I feel like I'm about to be on the wrong end of it, but his mouth descends on mine again and he kisses me slowly like he did before. Not the urgent desperation of last night that ended up in an all out fuck fest, though his hand is still cupped around my pussy. No, his kisses are slow and long and deep. That strange tongue glides alongside mine, tasting and teasing, discovering how I like to kiss, showing me what he wants in return.

Then his touch disappears, leaving me gasping and back on my own two feet. His name settles on the tip of my tongue, but I know better now than to call out. I wait instead, learning to peer at the moving shapes between the blank spaces in the darkness, how to read the air currents as they don't move, and the eddies when they do.

When his body presses to mind from behind, his Krampus form is complete, his cock pressed between my ass cheeks.

"I thought I'd be much sorer, the way you tore me apart," I confess, thinking back on last night, how I managed through my workday with no more than a few aches.

He huffs at the back of my neck, leaning down to lick a long path with his wet, warm tongue. "My saliva heals what it touches. You passed out, but I licked you head to toe. It also leaves my scent all over you."

"So you...marked me." I frown. "Aren't you supposed to ask before you do something like that?"

His arms slide around my waist, lifting me onto my toes against just with the bulk of him. "Little One, I bathed your pussy inside and out where otherwise you would have spent today crying, unable to fuck again tonight. Did you want that? Also, you came on me tonight," he adds as an almost after thought, though I don't buy the act. "And you taste like sweet rainwater and forest flowers."

"Oh." For once I have no comeback for that. "I'd

like to know what it feels like when you lick me," I whisper, glad the lights are off for the way my cheeks heat, though I miss seeing the glory of him in his monstrous form.

Not really thinking it through, I raise my hands over my head and run my fingers through his hair and along his horns, squeezing both gently in my palms.

And find myself on my knees, his hands wrapped tight around my wrists, breath hissing between his lips as he presses his cock to my mouth. "I fucking warned you, Little One. Open." Devlin releases one wrist to cup my jaw in his claws, tapping my cheeks with the dangerous points. "I won't say it again, but I will remove the option of breathing."

I part my lips and he surges forward, filling my mouth, my hair wrapped around his claws. My muffled cry becomes a gurgle. Devlin doesn't wait for me to suck in another breath before he slams his cock into my mouth over and over until my throat relaxes with the battering and I manage to take an inch of him there. With my throat plugged and full of cock, my nose almost pressing to his pubic hair for his length and my cheeks bulking with his girth, his claws cup my cheeks and throat and *squeeze.*

My panicked gurgle mingles with his anguished

groan as he fucks my throat with wild abandon, holding me in place. The schlucking noise fills my ears as he takes his pleasure and all I can do is be still and serve him.

A sense of power sweeps over me that all I have to do is massage his horns and he loses his shit. Leaning into his abuse and swallowing as gently as I can manage without gagging, though tears gather at the corners of my eyes and streak my cheeks, I wrap my arms around the back of his legs, pulling him in closer. A quick, rare breath through my nose and my body relaxes. Devlin's frantic pumping slows after a minute, though his claws knotted in my hair remain.

I sense him looking down at me and tip my head back as he draws back a little though not enough to leave my mouth empty. Sucking on the thick tip of him, I reach between his legs to play with his balls, earning another groan.

"Fuck, yes." His legs shake once his touch changes, cupping my head instead of driving my motions. "That's it."

He teaches me how he wants me to provide his pleasure and the most comes from giving him pleasure in return. Finally he reaches down and lifts me off the ground, settling me onto his hips.

"Thank you," I whisper, coughing a little. My voice won't come out any louder.

"I was rough with you, huh?" I sense the smile in his voice.

I nod, forgetting for a moment he can't see me. "Yes, you were rough. But I loved it."

"Good." His hand cracks down on my ass, first one side, then the other. "Hand around my neck. Stay off the horns. When I'm done, I'll fuck you, then lick you. Then you can have your picnic tomorrow. I promise. Safe word me if you need, okay?"

My brain goes fuzzy for the first few spanks trying to remember the damn safe word, but I don't end up using it. Sure, his spanks hurt, and sure my ass is on fire. But somewhere along the line Devlin and I established the one thing I never expected.

Trust.

And when he lifts me higher, gives me a searing kiss before drops me onto his cock, I scream myself raw for him, coming almost the second I coat him with my gushing fluids because I know he won't hurt me beyond what I can take.

Because he wants this too, just like I do.

When he grips my hips with those claws and pummels me frantically, faster than any human man could sustain, I scream in whispers into his shoulder, sobbing and crying against his flesh and never once let go of his neck, just as I promised.

And just as he promised, he carried me up to his bed afterward, his thick arms wrapped around me. Then he spreads my thighs and licks away the pain he causes until I shake and shudder and gush in his arms. Devlin bathes my skin with a degree of tenderness I know no other man will ever use to worship me. The bar has been set too high. He gives me every part of himself unreservedly.

My man is a Krampus. No one else will come close. Tomorrow we will go on our date, but I already know what my answer to our non-deal with my Christmas Krampus stalker will be.

"This is some dystopian hell you're teasing me with, Little One." Devlin reclines on my pink and blue picnic blanket, his face turned up to the sun, looking every inch the CEO citysider on Christmas Eve.

"You promised," I remind him, shaking an overpriced punnet of out of season berries one of the market vendors sold us along with a pair of hot apple ciders. "Go on," I coo, taking an inordinate amount of pleasure in his obvious discomfort.

"Daylight isn't my favorite," he mutters, taking one of the berries. The sting of his claws pinches the back of my fingers briefly in reprieve.

I grin at his brattiness. "At least here you can't molest me," I counter.

His gaze flickers to mine and locks on as he bites into the berry and swallows. "Don't tempt me."

Giggling, I cup my hands around the still steaming apple cider and sip the hot drink that slides down my throat. "That's so good."

"Mmhm."

I can't see his eyes, and it bothers me, but the one time I tried to remove his sunglasses, I earned myself a sharp scratch inside my wrist. Normally the pain wouldn't worry me—it's much less than anything else he's done. My legs still tremble at the memory of last night at his club. But the way he fixed me with a hard look and a set jaw stopped me from trying to remove the sunnies again.

"Nighttime is your domain, isn't it?"

"The darkness suits my...personality."

Swallowing the snort that wants to erupt, I opt to cuddle my drink instead, licking droplets from the rim of the plastic cup. "And what a personality."

"Are you going to tell me why we're here?"

"A testy little Krampus, aren't you?"

In an instant my cup is beside my head in the grass, and I'm half skewed off the blanket with his body arched over mine. To anyone else in the park we might look like a couple making out, but the fine vibrations passing through his taut frame tell me otherwise.

"I'm here at your bidding, Little One. Don't tease me." The tip of his tongue runs across his lips, and for a moment I think he might kiss me. Instead, he eases back to his original position, leaving me bereft of the contact I didn't realize how much I craved. The corners of his mouth quirk upward. "Regretting your choice of date activity?"

"Not in the least," I lie through my teeth. "Tell me what your brother was like as a child."

That stops him.

Devlin's head rotates on his neck like a puppeteer steers his actions. "My brother popped into existence as an adult, naked and paunched."

I stare for a moment. "With a beard," I add helpfully, as the ludicrous image solidifies in my mind.

"With a beard." Devlin nods.

"And you?"

A muscle plays in his jaw. It's sexy as hell. Not that he needs to know that.

"I...was younger."

"You mean you actually were a baby?" I tease.

"Perhaps. I don't remember."

My hand finds his, lacing our fingers together. "How old are you?"

Devlin shrugs. "What year is it?"

My mouth falls open. "You don't know what year it is?"

"Does it matter that much?" He slips his hand from mine, drawing his knees up into a vee. Long arms loop around them to clasp his opposite wrist.

That answers the age question, then.

I scoot a little closer. "What did you want to do, when you were a child?"

Devlin stills. "I thought we covered the child-hood angle already, Little One," he warns gently.

"I want to know who you are." Sucking on my bottom lip, I stare at him, a thousand thoughts running through my head.

What were you like with other women?

Who drove you away?

Were the last days a fluke? Our nights?

"You're asking about who I was." His back stiffens as I lean into his side.

"That's a part of you," I remind him.

"A part best forgotten, perhaps." Devlin shuts down.

"Gonna scratch your horns the next chance I get," I grumble.

"What was that?" His arm whips out around me, dragging me between his legs so my back presses to his chest. His arms slide around me, not caging, exactly. I mean, I'm not going anywhere, but he's holding me the way I hoped today's picnic would end.

"You're confusing me," I sigh, resting my head against his bicep that feels suspiciously hard beneath my cheek. "Are you, um, going to burst out into monster kind in public?"

His claws graze lightly across my ribs through my shirt, beneath my jacket. "Would that terrify you?"

"Only because you'd end up as a science experiment in some government lab or other," I murmur, my heart clenching because it's true.

"Ah. No pitchforks and fire, all knives and...other instruments?" he asks, sounding intrigued.

"You don't want to know. I think it'll make you angry."

His arms tighten around me. "No one is taking me away from you. I promise, Tanya." His lips rest briefly against my temple, then his chin rests on the top of my head. "Close your eyes. Sleep. You haven't had a lot of that in the last few nights."

My eyes drift shut in the sunshine on command, warmth and safety enclosing me on all sides. This isn't what I wanted to achieve from this date, but it's enough. A single thought flitters through my mind before exhaustion hits me on cue.

"Don't you sleep?"

His chest rumbles behind me. "Rest, Little One."

I'm out before I hear the rest of his answer.

CHAPTER NINE

DEVLIN

I leave Tanya asleep on her bed after our date on Christmas Eve on the night that should have been our fourth date and the closure of our deal. My win. Except that she never agreed to my deal.

And I'm not sure what she wants.

Hell, I'm not sure what I want.

And so I sit in the dark, drinking with the one person I shouldn't be with tonight, the one person who has a whole list of better things to do. Two of them, actually.

"She really has you knotted up, doesn't she?" Nick's voice holds the faintest hint of laughter even when he's sober.

Well, not entirely sober as we've been drinking

for the better part of two hours, but there's time. Plenty of it.

He gets those rounds done with hours to spare, because the bastard's hornier than a herd of Krampuses–*Krampusii?*—in a sex club without their little sub who purrs quietly on her own bed. The jolly red man creates plenty of mini offspring this time of year. Never thought how many babies are due at the end of June?

Instead of answering, I top us both up.

Nick raises his glass and downs it in one. "It's cheap and nasty."

"Like the shit you've always provided for me," I grouse.

He chuckles, the sound grating on my nerves. "Ah, she's your one, then."

"Looks like it."

"Be fucking happy, you old grump. Most people spend their entire lives looking for that one person."

"Then I've spent twenty-five of those durations in darkness."

"Yeah?" Nick's face reddens as he grins jovially at me. "So be fuckin' happy."

"You have no class," I mutter stiffly.

"And a whole lot of—"

"Stop." I press my hand to my temple. *Inviting him was a mistake.* "Go back to your day job."

"Only one more night before I get to have a little siesta."

"Don't mix your cultures."

A migraine brews at the back of my mind. I should have stayed with Tanya, waited at the edge of her bed to torment her the moment she woke up. Better yet, I could bring her back here and tease her some more. The club isn't open for the next two nights. Executive decision, unpopular with the staff, but they can blow me.

Figuratively.

It's Tanya, or no one.

The thought of another female's hands on my cock leaves me wanting to strip my skin from my bones.

Both sets.

I flick my phone out of my pocket.

Devlin: Are you awake, Little One?

I wait, but not three dots appear, and the message doesn't go to read.

> **Devlin:** I enjoy wearing you out. Come to the club.

> **Devlin:** Let me play games with your mind, Tanya. Let me tease you.

Her lack of response irritates me, but then I forget how much humans need their rest. She barely responded to me as I carried her in through her window, figuring the cafe goers might have something to say about the strange man taking the girl who lived alone always up her stairs unconscious in my arms.

But she was awake enough to kiss me back languidly, enough to stoke my desire until I came within an inch of stripping her bare and fucking her slowly on top of her bed like we did the first night, just on a different speed setting.

Something about the trust in her sleepy eyes, the sweet caress of her finger on my cheek in human form gave me pause. She insisted on that schmozzle of a date this afternoon in the damned sunlight for a reason. I still hadn't fathomed that out, but whatever her reasons, she intended no sex was a part of it.

And since she wasn't quite lucid when I brought her home, I kept to my promise, kissing her sweetly as I laid her back and covered her with her blankets, ticking her in before I slipped back out the way I came, the general populace none the wiser that I'd ever been in her room at all.

Then I returned to my own home above the club and drank myself stupid, both before and after my big brother arrived to help with my efforts.

Finally, Nick pushes up to his feet, lumbering only slightly. "Should probably do the rest of the hemisphere," he acknowledges. "Got some of the housewives who rely on regular appearances, and all."

I raise an eyebrow, noting vaguely that my cheeks lost feeling a while back. "And the children. Are you alright to drive?"

"Dancer knows the route by heart. All I have to do is hold on." He shrugs on his coat, leaving a trail of pale glitter all over my floor.

I hate it. Tanya will love it.

"Bon voyage, then."

"Didn't you just tell me not to mix my

languages?" He squints my way and holds out his arms. "Hug?"

"Not really in the mood." I rise anyway and step toward him, letting the giant of a beast of a man who folds himself around me. We're of a height, though even in my true form I'm still a third of his girth. "Don't pull the seat out of your pants this year on chimney stacks."

He laughs at the old reminder. "Ah, that was a good year. Elves never have forgotten." His face sobers. "Go see her, brother. Call me when you need, yes? I'll drop everything for you."

My face cracks with the rare ability to smile. "Even on your day off?"

"Especially on my day off." He kisses both of my cheeks and slaps me familiarly, then he's gone, leaving more fucking glitter on my black carpets.

"Asshole," I mutter with no venom in it, checking my phone.

She still hasn't replied. My brother's words echo through my mind, and I raise my eyes to my older paraphernalia I brought with me out of the cave when I reemerged into the world. My leather pants and jacket hang behind my desk chair, still supple from a lot of TLC I put into them after I bought the club. Who knew a few old, large gems and a chest full of gold would be worth so much sixteen hundred years or so years later?

The last item leaning in the corner of the black painted room—I had a theme in mind, alright?—is a bundle of birch sticks, each lovingly collected, each stripped down, bent under a running stream for flexibility, endurance. Perfect for a certain activity that leaves one's behind stinging with the pain of a thousand bee stings.

If she won't reply to me and begs for pain, I'll deliver to her the present she deserves.

Right before I claim her permanently.

"Wakey wakey," I coo as I trail my claws along Tanya's window, relishing the sound that ruins the night's serenity.

The cafe below her apartment closed hours before, the plethora of last Christmas shoppers dispersing while I waited in my usual spot across the road. My single mistake in leaving her earlier was to close the drapes. I can't see her, and that lack of visual cue alone has left me on edge for the past two hours, waiting for a suitable break in local traffic to re-enter her apartment.

A twisted smile curves my lips as my horns extend, the clothes I donned for my picnic with her stretched to their limit by the time I raise her window, couching in full sight in my demonic form as I stare at her bed.

Her empty bed.

"Little one," I murmur, jumping down and prowling across the room, my collection of bound birch sticks in hand, adding an extra lash for every step I take across the threadbare carpet.

After this, she's moving out of this shitty life of hers and in with me. The coffee shop, with its permanent aroma of burnt beans and sour cakes, has to go. "Come on out."

I reach the bathroom door and tap its already scarred surface with my claw, adding to its plethora of marks. *Definitely time for an upgrade.* The door swings inward revealing...

Nothing.

I frown. The room is as empty as her bed. Pivoting on my heel I wander her room, quelling the panic rising in my chest with every step. And with every step I'm not sure if I'm adding another lash to her count...

Or if I'm subtracting one.

Finally, I stop by her bed, smoothing my claws

back into my human form. The divot in her blankets where I left her is still slightly depressed. Residual heat remains. *Not long, then.* Not caring how stupid I look, I crouch and peer beneath her bed.

I need her eyes to peer back at me. Her feet wiggle away as she giggles and runs from me. Oh, the chase to catch her—

But that shadowed space, too, is empty.

My chest clenches down as I stride to her door, my hand on the lock as my clawed feet kick something small, cold and what most definitely shouldn't be there at all.

Her phone.

Stomach acid rises to my throat as I flip the device in my fingers and input her passcode. One of the first things I did when I bought the club was hire myself a techspert—my own term, not hers—and educated myself about this new world, its inner workings, finances and how to hack every part of it.

I never played by the rules before. There's no reason to change my habits in this century.

Scrolling through her apps—none of them organized in any regular order, everything chaotic, like her—I find her messages and open the top one.

No spoiler that it's not mine.

. . .

Samson: You went on a second date with that monster.

Samson: I saw you.

Samson: I'll take you somewhere better than he did.

I roll my eyes. Samson needs to get a life. Her lack of responses speaks volumes. *My Little One remains loyal to me.* Some of the bile retreats from my tongue and the pressure in my chest loosens, at least until I read the next line.

Samson: If you want restraints, I'll cage you where no one will hear your screams.

Tanya: Fuck off, psycho.

Tanya: There's a reason we didn't have a second date.

Samson: I'll see you soon.

Tanya: Blocking now.

．　．　．

That's the end of the conversation. No matter how I scroll through, check her calls, anything, there's no more. Either she blocked him after that, or he gave up.

But judging from her empty room, her dropped phone she never is without, the ache in my chest...

I don't think so.

Tracking back to her bed, I close my eyes, lean down and inhale deeply. Tanya's sweet scent of night jasmine and rainwater fills my senses, mingling with a bitter tang of something that draws on a deeper level of disquiet inside me.

Someone else has been here. Worse than that, it's someone I know.

Samson's name is bullshit. But the best part is, I know exactly where to find the fucker.

Grabbing my bundle of birch sticks I leap from the window, channeling my form into one I rarely use that my big brother is so fond of, though my path leaves no trace of pretty sparkles in its wake.

Mine is of soot and vengeance.

CHAPTER TEN

TANYA

My world is reduced to the spaces between eight uneven bars. I woke here, stripped bare or maybe Devlin never dressed me again after he took me home. But it's not Devlin who stole me away from the warmth of my safe, locked staircase. My vision doesn't reach beyond the base of a black, plastic covered bed that no one occupies, though cuffs dangle from the corners, pristine and unused looking. Like the cage. The whole room.

All that's missing is a camera and some lights. Maybe a sleazy director.

But that's not who sits across the room from me. The man who, when I dated him, called himself Samson. But when Devlin handed him our coats at his club the night he took me to his safe space, he used another name.

Beau.

I only saw a sliver of him then, but I did see his shirt bearing the same logo that was on Devlin's desk when he carried me through his office on the way to his bed. The same logo on Beau's shirt now. I didn't connect anything at the time but now I've had what feels like hours in this cramped, cold cage to come to terms with the fact that I'm in a whole lot of trouble that maybe even my Krampus can't fix.

A shiver ripples across my skin I try not to show, digging my fingers into the cement floor that grounds me. My toes hit the small drain grill in the center of the floor beneath me, and a sob breaks free.

Beau's mouth splits into a gaping smile.

"He played with you, didn't he? In both forms?" He doesn't wait for an answer or even look for one. Grandstanding to an audience of one, right there. A captive audience at Christmas. No puns. This is as psychotic as it gets. I don't know if we're at the club, or if we're somewhere else, like his home. It doesn't matter.

Devlin wasn't there when I woke up to another man in my room, and we never did agree on a deal.

The picnic ended...strangely. I wish I'd just stuck with the sex caveat. That seemed to be his safe place. But no, I had to go out on a limb and push for more, try to dig into the hardened heart of a creature over fifteen hundred years old. And, why? To satisfy my own curiosity? He would have answered my questions in time if I just gave him what he wanted and now....

I'm here. Without him.

With this psycho. Who is still. Fucking. Talking.

"I don't understand why you want that monster? Is it the claws? The horns? Does he have a bigger dick?" Beau carries on, unbuttoning his shirt as his attention slides away from me to a mirror at the side of the room where he studies the man on the other side.

It really is taking narcissism to another level.

"A bit of all of those, really. But I do love the horns," I say absently.

If I'm going to die, my new life goal is to make this man feel as small as possible. For every inch of fear I feel I channel it into hurting the reflection he covets.

Suicidal, remember?

Beau swivels back to face me. The girl in the cage. "I'm sure I can find enough toys to break you, split you apart. Don't worry, sweetheart. I'll make it a bloody Christmas morning. You can drip all over his bed. And when he comes home after he scours the city for you, gets drunk with his brother and tears your shitty little cafe house apart, he'll find you here."

I bare my teeth though my legs wobble and I'm glad I'm curled on the floor. And of the drain that scares the shot out of me, because I'm not sure if I just wet myself out of fear.

So that's what the drain is for.

Then it hits me that this is Devlin's room, and his drain.

Somehow, that concept lessens the fear a little, gives me hope. *Maybe he'll come back.*

Beau crouches by my cage, a delirious smile etched across his face. "It was just a chance that I worked for him, you know. You've been my obsession for nearly two years, since we started talking online. Do you remember, Tanya? You shared a clip with me. Stuffing your pussy with toys. Said you wished you could have bigger ones, let them bruise and batter you. Do you remember?" he croons lovingly, his face a twisted mess.

I shiver, unable to suppress this one, and back to the furthest reaches of the cage. "He'll come back."

"No, sweetheart. He won't." Beau reaches a thick finger through the bars and taps my nose condescendingly. "After all that teasing, we had one coffee date. *One date*," he spits, his voice rising to a screech. "You never let me show you what I could do for you. How I can do what you need. You didn't have to let that monster into your cunt. I can batter you," he promises, his eyes lighting with sickening fervor again.

I shake my head. "You're so wrong. This is pathetic. You know he'll kill you."

"He has no idea where you are, or who I am." Beau stands, stepping outside my field of vision, and wheels something squeaky towards my cage. A black slinky cloth that looks like it might have once suited Devlin's bed covers the thing beneath that stands hip height to the giant ex-doorman to my Krampus' club.

Beau's hand flicks the cloth away with a flourish. I'm left looking at a machine I've only ever seen before in dirty movies. Mechanical, intimidating to start, it's a fucking machine with two dildoes attached. It makes sense that Devlin would have something like it in the club, or even for his personal use with playdates. The thought of playing with others hurts, so I push that vision aside and fixate on the terror inches from my nose instead.

It's a mistake.

The dildos could be measured on a Krampus. Actually, I know exactly who they are measured on, and it hits me just how important his oral worship aftercare is to my continued sanity.

Without him...

The ramifications of the messages sent to tease and torment a date I never intended to capitulate on hit me in full. I scramble to the back of the cage as Beau pushes the machine forward, securing it to the floor.

"Oh, no, darling. I'll take your life on his bed, not down there. The mess will be up here. Give me just a second—"

An eternity passes as clanks reverberate the floor. I reach down and press against the cement, frowning. *Cement.* Devlin's room was on the second—or maybe third—story of the club.

This isn't his room.

It might be a lower dungeon set up to *look* like Dev's room, but it is not his. I breathe out a sigh that brings another sob with it. Beau laughs, thinking he has me by the victorious sound that ricochets around the room, the echo bouncing from wall to wall. A second thought slams into me as I raise my eyes to his.

"You know nothing of monsters. You're not even a real one," I whisper, fear fully thinning my voice to almost nothing. I force the words past my lips, making sure they come out clearly, making sure he hears them. "He'll destroy you."

Beau snarls, a pathetic sound. A laugh leaves me even as he launches at the cage, rattling the metal contraption where it sits. The metal scrapes the flooring beneath the force of his weight, slamming me backward. My neck snaps, my skull contacting the bars, and I smile as the world narrows to a singular point of black haze.

I know I'm right.

Beau might steal my life, but I'll make sure my Krampus knows exactly who took from him. It's the last gift I can give to the monster I love.

CHAPTER ELEVEN

DEVLIN

I slide down the club's chimney like I'm fucking Santa Claus on Christmas morning, ready to deliver presents. Only Beau won't enjoy this gift, though I will, once I dig my claws into him.

Not a euphemism, in case the nuance is missed there.

My office and my adjoining bedroom is empty, as is the auditorium I played with Tanya in the other night. I stall in the hallway outside, wondering not for the first time if I haven't read the situation completely wrong. That she doesn't want me, hasn't run from me.

That they didn't plan this together and left at her bidding.

My chest cramps as I slump against the hall wall, gripping my birch bundle in one hand, her cardigan in my other. The scent of her fuels my obsessive need. Even if I have got it wrong, who's to say his obsession isn't worse than mine? Then I recall the way she blew him off in the message.

No. She's not with him willingly. I hope. Damn, I hope. My fist slams through the wall at my side, leaving a Krampus-sized hole. I'll have the staff fix it tomorrow. Fuck, tomorrow is Christmas. Maybe another day, as we're shut for a few more.

My leather pants and vest flex as I stride along the black carpeted corridor. The old clothes seemed the right attire for tonight's work.

"Housewives were a lot less trouble than this in the day," I grouse, though I'm not angry at her. Well, I am if she runs from me. Though I don't think that's the case.

I hope so.

Fuck. I roar my insanity to the black walled hallway, and nothing echoes back.

Closing my eyes I release a ragged breath and head for the alley door I entered through last time with her. I know his home address. It's where I should have headed first. Some instinct drew me back to the club, despite the words in his message. I thought they might have been an attempt at misdirection, but I over thought that.

Apparently I'm more devious than her kidnapper.

I push the door open as a tinny echo of my roar filters back to me from the bowels of the club that drill three levels below the street. My brow dips. The halls are soundproofed, like the upper floors for neighbor's sanity and public peace.

That shouldn't be possible.

Closing the door with infinite gentleness and shutting out the early hours of Christmas morning before the sun rises, I turn back to the innards of my club and dissipate into the stuff nightmares are made of.

If she's here, I'll find her.

Four rooms and three stairwells later, I find the room she's in, tied to a bed with a plastic cover as though he's prepared to sacrifice her to a false god who will never accept his offering.

Though if we reverse their placements, I'll happily take him instead.

She's never looked more beautiful, bound to the bed, spread out on display. Pity it's for an asshole who won't live to breathe in the glory he's created for that much longer. One hundred breaths, though he doesn't know his time is so limited.

I slip through the darkened room on the echo of her fading scream to murmur sweet everythings in her ear.

"Count for me, Little One."

"One, two, th-three…" Her screams turn to sobs, her hands shaking in their bonds.

Only I know they're tears of relief.

Beau, the fuckwit on a reduced life span, looks down at her like she's the craziest one in the room. "Are you praying for more time, sweetheart?"

Wrong, fucker.

"—Eleven, twelve—"

Her cracked whisper fills me with the sort of joy I've craved from the moment I saw her. I did promise her I had sadistic tendencies. Her tears are my greatest turn on, but only when they're for me and the ones she cries now are the prettiest offering I've ever seen.

I'll reward her later, in the upper levels. After I torch this room like the lowest echelon of hell.

"—twenty-four, twenty-five—"

The unending trust she provides as he positions that machine between her legs is of the heart wrenching variety. My claws are the first part of me to flash back into existence as I slash them across his throat.

Hot fluids add to the darkness of this room, spraying her with my atonement for leaving her this afternoon.

"You shouldn't have touched that which is mine," I whisper while Beau's brain still has some function.

"—thirty-seven, thirty-eight—"

Before she counts to forty, the man I trusted bleeds out over the foot of the plastic covered bed. Did I say one hundred? I'm a bad liar. Or an impatient one.

Crouching at her feet, I kiss my way along her legs, kicking the machine back away from her as I slither along her body, little more than a mouth, claws and thighs as I press over her. The rest of me is smoke, until I encounter her heat.

Then, I find I'm not as insubstantial as I thought as I soak my cock in her fluids, sinking balls deep as I kiss her long and deep.

"I'm sorry, Little One. I would never let him hurt you with those plastic fake cocks."

"Inappropriate." She giggles breathlessly between moans and gasps, her body clenching down on my cock even as her hips rock up to meet my shallow thrusts. "This isn't normal," she moans.

"You're right." I nod decisively, leaning into her, earning another moan, and lash out with one taloned foot, decapitating her unalived assailant. "Now, we can fuck. And I can apologize to the woman I love."

Her eyes flare wide. "You love me?" Wonder reflects starlight in the depths of her mortal soul, and I promise she'll never want for anything, every day of that life.

"I love you." I kiss her slowly, reaching up to free her hands, slicing all four bonds with my talons and claws. The cuffs still dangle from her wrists, but that doesn't matter as she wraps her limbs around me, clinging close. "I love you and want to spend this life with you."

"Alright." Another sob, no conditions, no deals.

She agrees.

My roar fills the club's levels, all of them, as I rail into her stunning body, claiming her as mine, coating us both in the blood of the sacrifice I offer at her feet for my sins.

Her acceptance clamps around my cock as she reaches up to slide her palms along my horns, and I fill her womb with the seed of my stain, desperate to meld our souls, needing her closer than this fleshy form allows.

When she screams so beautifully for me, crying and sobbing in uncontrollable bursts as she comes and cries and breaks and shatters, I bathe her in my tongue. We have all the time, every remaining night hour to remove the stain of his touch from her.

Then I carry her to my room as I promised, sealing the dungeon and torching it. I'll scrub the walls with acid after, but that can wait.

For now, I have a ceremony I need performed, and there's only one person I'll trust with this duty.

CHAPTER TWELVE

TANYA

I'm married to a horned monster on Christmas Day by Santa Claus.

The only dress Devlin deemed suitable in the club, after discarding a white nurse's outfit—just—is a white latex gown that drapes to the floor in elegant folds he polished himself to a high shine. Long, thigh high white boots encase my legs, though I wear no underwear whatsoever, and a halter neck bodice encases my breasts to perfection. The latex molds to my flesh he spent way too much time on, tugging at my nipples until I became a moaning, hot mess beneath his ministrations.

Elbow length white gloves complete the look.

Devlin speculatively handed me a ball gag, but that one is on the table as a maybe after treat. *Maybe.*

Before I met him, I never thought of getting married, and I'd never tried latex on. It's surprisingly comfortable and the way he worshiped me, the dedication he offered polishing each section took literal hours. I've never felt so loved in my life.

Ours has been a whirlwind romance, the Krampus and the human. And here I stand before his brother, St. Nicholas, in his red fuzzy suit, beard and all, and two elves who yawn every time someone pokes them after a hard night's work.

The one thing I never knew about Santa Claus? The man is a sex friend. And he's most definitely a boob man. Throughout the ceremony, his gaze never left mine and his fingers attempted to wander on more than one occasion. Devlin keeps that in check, too.

Finally we hit the *I do* part, which is good because I haven't really been listening and I get the impression that Dev would have hurried the whole situation along but despite only having one day off for the whole year, or so Nick informed me, he appears to be in no hurry to get his formal duty over and done with.

"I do," I repeat after Dev, who wastes no time,

cupping his hand around the back of my neck and slamming his mouth over mine in a filthy kiss that leaves me wet and panting in his arms. His tongue splits, entwining mine until it feels like I'm kissing two men at once. I pull back, gasping, my face heated and sneak a look at Nick.

He watches me with hooded eyes. "If you need help with peeling the latex off, at all..." he offers, not a playful tone evident in his voice.

"Thanks, but we're good." Devlin grips me tight, marring the work he did earlier but I don't think he cares for the fact his claws dig into my side, and I know he'll shred the latex the second we're alone.

"Alright then. If you're sure?" Nick wiggles an eyebrow at me.

One of his elves huffs, grabs his master's coat and jingles his hat bell. The three of them disappear and then it's just Dev and myself in his office, and a certificate that magically fills itself in with golden ink and our names.

"Thank fuck," Dev growls, pulling me flush to his leather clad body.

He alone refused to change after the mess downstairs. He *did* let me clean his body with a towel, watching me with hooded eyes as I knelt, and I know what I want to do now before he ruins the dress he spent so long worshiping me in.

"Is that the formalities," I whisper, tracing my palm down the inside of his open vest where his Krampus skin is all hard ridges and sexy swirls and patterns.

"All down. You're mine now, Little One. Forever."

"And you're mine." I knock his hand away before he can thwart me and slide to my knees, licking my way down.

Breath hisses between his teeth as I mouth the leather front of his pants. "Can I please?"

He helps me unlace the leather, showing me how the intricate knots work, and frees his gorgeous cock to my eyes. I swear I salivate on the spot.

Devlin taps my cheek with his cock head thoughtfully. "Open, Tanya."

I open my lips wide and he pushes in, all the way to the back of my throat. I know he wants my tears and so I impale myself deeper, offering my pain freely. A groan leaves him as he wraps his hands in my hair and pushes my head down onto him roughly.

The noise that releases from my throat humiliates me and I'm so glad the color stains my cheeks when he thickens in my mouth, evidence that he takes pleasure in my embarrassment. Drool runs down my chin when I can't take him all. His hand flexes a warning on the back of my head before he fucks my mouth brutally.

Those claws grip my head and draw me up his body. My mouth aches, my knees sting. I blink dozily at him as he wipes my mouth tenderly with those same claws, cradling me to his body.

"Lost you there for a moment, Little One," he murmurs.

"Did you?" I lean in for a kiss and he lets me, going slow and tender.

My heart wants to burst, and the sobs start fresh as he lifts me against his body. "Today will be a lot." His mouth presses sweetly to mine. "Will you let me break you, and I promise I'll reward you after?"

"That wasn't a reward just then?" I frown at him when he laughs at me.

"Oh, my perfect one." His arms tighten. "Forgive me."

Those claws slash my dress to slivers. I stare down at it. "I loved the way you polished me," I mutter, uncurling the strips from my breasts.

"I hated the way my brother looked at you like he wanted to devour you," he growls.

My head jerks up. "I didn't want him to—"

"I know." He shushes me with kisses. "I want to spank you. Will you let me?" His cock presses against my heat.

"While you're inside me?" My brow dips, my mind trying to work out his angle.

His laugh catches me off guard, then I'm airborne, high above the floor and his bed, floating in his arms like smoke, and his form solidifies *within* me.

I scream at the sudden intrusion as he reforms behind me, already impaling me on his monster cock.

"What an idea," he murmurs as his hand comes down on my rump again and again and again, warming my flesh. Claws grip my skin as he fucks me frantically, the monstrous noises from him terrifying and arousing.

And as my orgasm peaks, he kisses me and—

We plummet.

All the way to the bed.

Devlin fucks into me the moment we land, deeper than I thought possible, melding us together. My mind fractures, leaving me with enough space to wonder if it will always be like this, with my immortal monster, bonded to a human, forever.

Because if it is—
I'm okay with that.

EPILOGUE

DEVLIN

I give her a week's reprieve before I bring out the birch sticks. Her mouth opens in a pretty little 'o' shape. I instantly want to stuff my cock inside, but that's not what tonight is for. I let her distract me on our wedding night with that mouth, and her idea that ended up being the best memory of my twisted, fucked up existence, but she won't have a second chance.

After a week of cleaning up the bottom levels, expunging the spirit of the deceased with a full exorcism and giving the walls a personal acid bath, I reopened the club with a new complement of staff, each of whom have signed a full NDA and a few of their rights away, though they don't seem to mind as they get full club membership and a few other perks.

Now, my little wife is spread out over a spanking horse—padded, of course, I'm not a complete barbarian—her wrists and calves strapped down, knees spread astride and cunt dripping for me.

Not that I'll be playing with that little hole for a while tonight.

I stroke the birch bundle along her spine, reveling in her delicious shiver. The anticipation is almost as good as the pain. *Almost*.

But not quite.

"Are you ready?"

"Yes, please." Her breaths already shallow, she clenches her thighs on the horse that does nothing to alleviate the pressure building over her sensitive places.

"Oh, is my Little One dripping for me? I might not even fuck that hole tonight. Such a pity." She mewls delightfully, her sounds intensifying—if muted, somewhat—when I wrap the pretty ball gag I had out for our wedding and buckle it behind her head, stroking her hair sweetly. "What was that safe word again?"

She sobs softly, knowing I won't take her no for

an answer today, though the scent of her need soaks into my furniture.

"So beautiful. Little One." I stroke over her buttocks with the birch, letting her get used to the feel before I take them away and give no warning whatsoever before I strike her.

Tanya's scream is muted, and close to endless in this room that's set inside another chamber. That one is soundproofed.

This, however, is not.

Set up to look like a medieval torture chamber, the walls are built of actual stone. The engineers had fun exploring the weight of that on the second floor. But it passed inspection, and has the most wonderful acoustics.

The next few strikes leave my arm in a flurry. Pretty marks decorate her thighs and her sumptuous rump as she cries for me. Swallowing hard and ready to slam myself hilt deep in her sopping cunt, I place the birch on the bench in front of her, where she can see the instrument of her punishment, and lean in to whisper in her ear.

"Do you remember begging me for pain, Little One?" A nod. "Do you wish you could take it back now?" I lick at her tears as they flow so beautifully.

Tanya shakes her head, moaning when I reward

her with a sharp breath and a finger in her pussy. I add a second, pumping into her until she's close to her first orgasm of the night then yanks my hand free, slapping her soaked, slick flesh with my wet hand, following up with a flurry of strikes. If she can come from the pain, she's welcome to it. Otherwise I'll bring her to the edge, and drop her back.

Repeat.

Over and over we turn the cycle until her cries weaken and even her moans are the sweetest, softest whispers.

Only then do I unlace my leather pants, free my cock and slide into her hot, clenching depths. "So desperate to be filled, little wife." I cup the back of her neck, massaging gently as I ream myself into her slicked hole.

She tips her head to the side, laying her cheek on the leather padding and surrenders.

I've never seen anything more beautiful in my life. All sixteen hundred and fifty-eight years of existence.

My cock pulses in her cunt. I rail her, pinning her in place with my claws, and brand her with my seed. A hot flush ripples through her as she comes with me, milking me dry a second time until my orgasm almost hurts.

Panting, I withdraw my cock from her dripping hole and wipe my seed on her reddened buttocks. She winces slightly even as I harden against the sight, resting my cock in the crack of her ass and rubbing gently.

A lifetime with one woman. I've never spent more than a single night once a year with anyone, and even then I was lucky not to spend more than two years turning around.

Huh. Something else I have in common with the human who captured the attention of a Krampus and tethered me to her.

Smiling stupidly, I lean in to kiss along her flesh as I unbuckle her wrists and ankles, licking across her skin in soothing motions. Her ass wiggles and I raise an eyebrow.

"What more can you take tonight, Little One?"

Her answer is perfectly her, perfectly us.

"Everything you need."

Fuck if I won't love her for an eternity.

Thank you for reading Devlin and Tanya's Christmas
Monster Brides story!
Please leave a review for your favorite Krampus here.
If you haven't read my other works in this series
check out:
KRAKEN'S VOW
PHOENIX'S ETERNAL FLAME

ABOUT THE AUTHOR

Raven Hush writes paranormal & BDSM romance and exists on a diet of red wine and coffee. When she isn't romancing the monster under her bed, she writes contemporary romance and suspense as *USA Today bestselling* author Sofia Aves and kidlit under a not-so-super-secret pen name. Raven lives near Brisbane, Australia, with her three crazies and two German shepherds who like to pose whilst wrestling. Raven writes in her own dragon bookish cave and wrangles her alpacas daily. One day, she might even write about them.

Bookishly stalk Raven:
WEBSITE
AMAZON
BOOKBUB
INSTAGRAM
TWITTER
FACEBOOK

ALSO BY RAVEN HUSH

CLUB FRAY

PURGE

DARKEST DESIRES

KIDNAPPED BY CLAWS

RUIN

MONSTER BRIDES

PHOENIX'S ETERNAL FLAME

KRAKEN'S VOW

KRAMPUS' CHRISTMAS BRIDE

SILENT SENTINELS

REFLECTIONS OF SILENCE

ECHOES IN THE VOID